I0631142

E. B. Crisman

The Scriptural Argument on the Mode of Baptism in a Nut-Shell

E. B. Crisman

The Scriptural Argument on the Mode of Baptism in a Nut-Shell

ISBN/EAN: 9783337392697

Printed in Europe, USA, Canada, Australia, Japan

Cover: Foto ©Andreas Hilbeck / pixelio.de

More available books at **www.hansebooks.com**

THE SCRIPTURAL ARGUMENT

ON THE

MODE OF BAPTISM

IN A NUT-SHELL.

BY E. B. CRISMAN, D. D., O
Of the Cumberland Presbyterian Church.

ST. LOUIS, MO.:
Printed for the Author by
RYAN, JACKS & CO., 602 N. FOURTH STREET.
1880.

Entered according to Act of Congress, in the year 1880, by
E. B. CRISMAN, D. D., in the Office of Librarian of Congress,
at Washington, D. C.

CONTENTS.

THE MODE OF BAPTISM.

CHAPTER I.

INTRODUCTION.

As introductory to this book, the reader's attention is asked to the following statements:

1. This is no exhaustive treatise nor elaborate discussion. It seeks to cover the entire field of Scriptural argument by giving simply a compendium of the leading heads. It is intended to aid families and young persons in getting, in a nutshell, the true Scriptural doctrine on the subject discussed. Young ministers will find in it an assistant for their own use and one which may be safely, and it is believed profitable, put into the hands of intelligent young converts who may find themselves vexed on this vexacious question.

2. The author does not claim originality in the arguments here given. A great many books have been read and arguments from

them freely used. To make a formal acknowl-
edgement on the many pages where free use
has been made of the thoughts of others,
would be to print a great deal of technical
matter which would be of no service to the
reader and for which he cares nothing. The
book used more than all others together was
the Holy Bible, to which credit is given in
every instance.

3. The occasion for sending forth this book
is the same which has existed for many genera-
tions — nothing more, nothing less. Immersionists, assuming that there can be no controversy as to the Scriptural mode of baptism,
have boldly and noisily proceeded to declare
the remainder of the Christian world without a
church or church relations, and without the
requisite qualifications for the sacrament of the
Lord's Supper. They are doing the same
thing yet. This book, therefore, is put forth on
the ground of self-defence, as are many others
of a similar kind. Pædobaptist ministers feel
that they have more important and welcome
messages to deliver from the pulpit than fre-
quent discussions on this non-essential; but as

their silence is misconstrued by their noisy opponents, they deem it best to put their defence and arguments in handy books which the intelligent and pious may quietly and prayerfully read.

4. This book has no proselyting design and the reader, whoever he or she may be, is hereby kindly requested not so to use it. Many Immersionists compass sea and land to make one convert to their mode; indeed it seems that some of them will labor more and make more sacrifice to accomplish this than to convert a sinner from the error of his way and save a soul from hell; and will exult more over the proselyte than over the convert. But we beg our readers to have a higher and holier aim. Read for information and use that for spiritual comfort, for usefulness, and for heavenly and eternal exultation and triumph. And may the Lord help you.

5. This is not intended to be either a learned or a critical discussion. If any critic should wish to criticise the language, rhetoric or logic of this book, or any Immersionist essay to reply to it, let him criticise and reply. The author's

time and attention are otherwise employed,
and such persons will receive no notice from
him.   His work is done when the book is prepared and circulated.   It is supposed to be able
to defend itself.

CHAPTER II.

IMMERSIONISTS — ARE THEY BAPTISTS ? — THE ISSUE.

1. *Defined.* Immersionists are those Christians who practice the mode of water baptism defined by Alexander Campbell in these words : " We must *dip* only once, and the motion must be *backwards.*" Three things are declared essential : 1st. *Dipping.* 2nd. Only *one* motion, or dipping. 3rd. This motion must be *backwards*, or face up. On this definition of what they erroneously claim to be *the* Scriptural water baptism, we understand the so called Baptist churches all to agree. This definition requires that the subject be applied to the water, instead of the water to the subject — and that in a method with prescribed details as above.

The Greek Church maintain that the subject must be plunged three times, and after these three immersions must be *sprinkled* with water. They have two of the prescribed essentials, viz : the *dipping,* and the *backward* motion ; but not

the *"only once."* And besides, they *sprinkle.*
Of course, then the Greek Church cannot be
classed with Immersionists.

The *Dunkards* not only insist on a triple immersion, but also that it be by a *forward* motion or face down. Thus they have only one
of the prescribed essentials, viz: the *dipping;*
and are without two, viz: the *"only once"* and
the *"backward"* motion. And on the contrary they dip three times and the face down.
So they too cannot be classed with Immersionists.

2. *Their Numbers.* Of the sixty or seventy
millions of Protestants of all denominations in
the world, probably not a *fiftieth* part have been
baptized by immersion. Dr. Kurtz, of the
Lutherian Church, a careful author, says,
"probably not *one-sixtieth* part practice submersion." The proportion of the Christian
world, who practice immersion, is *very* small.
This is mentioned for information; not as an
argument.

3. *Their Assumptions.* They claim: First,
that immersion, as above defined, is the Scriptural and only mode of water baptism. Second-

ly, that in baptism the mode is the ordinance; and if the mode is altered, the ordinance is abolished. Thirdly, then all who are not immersed are unbaptized. Fourthly, that the unbaptized have no rights at the Lord's table; hence: Strict or Close-Communion. Fifthly, that there is no Church but an immersing and immersed Church. Sixthly, the unimmersed are living out of the Church and out of the line of duty. Seventhly, if out of the Church and the line of duty "there is no promise to them."

4. *The Issue.* As already stated, Immersionists hold, first, that in baptism the subject is to be applied to the water by being dipped into it backwards; second, that this precise mode of its performance is essential to the presence of the ordinance; third, that *dipping* the subject into water, or applying him to the water, is the only Scriptural (mode of) baptism. On the contrary Pædobaptists as firmly maintain, first, that the precise mode of the performance is not essential to the presence or validity of the ordinance: second, that applying the water to the subject is the Scriptural mode of baptism.

The Cumberland Presbyterian and other Presbyterian Confessions of Faith say, " Dipping of the person into the water is not necessary; but baptism is rightly administered by pouring, or sprinkling water, upon the person." Pres. Con. Faith; Chap. XXVIII, Sec. III.

I am aware that some have erroneously interpreted this language of the Con. of Faith to allow the validity and even the propriety of immersion and only to claim that the performance by affusion is valid baptism. But I understand it to be a plain and positive declaration that affusion is the *right*, because the *Scriptural*, mode of baptism, and that immersion is not right.

Attention is asked to the following remarks on the above:

1. Among the comparatively few Christians who advocate submersion there are many conflicting opinions as to the precise mode of its performance. Among those who practice sprinkling there are no such conflicting opinions.

2. The Immersionists—being only, say, the *one-fiftieth* part—boldy unchurch the whole of the Christian world besides, their fellow-submersionists as well, and strongly intimate to the

other *forty-nine-fiftieth* part that they have no promise of heaven. They must be honest in this, or else they would not do what seems to the great body of the Christian world arrogant and unreasonable. But their honesty certainly must be confined to the interpretation of one passage of the Scripture only, viz. : " Strait is the gate, and narrow is the way, * * and *few there be* that find it." Matt. vii, 14.

3. Thus mankind are confronted with the spectacle of a very small proportion of the Christian world, who, while loudly repudiating all *written* creeds, have adopted an *unwritten* one, which is by far the narrowest one of this age, and have made it the exacting rule by which *one* is allowed to pronounce upon the Christian order of *forty-nine* and to declare them without a church and church privileges and blessings, and very nearly, if not quite, without any well-founded hope of heaven ! " Whom the gods would destroy they first make mad."

4. It is the purpose to prove in this book that Sprinkling, meaning the application of the water to the subject, is the Scriptural mode of per-

forming the act of baptism. If this be true, Immersionists not only have not an exclusive right to the name *Baptist*, but have not an equal right to it with Pædobaptists. As the latter practice the mode of performance according to the Scripture, they are the true Scriptural *Baptists*. Hence our opponents will be distinguished by the name *Immersionists*, as this discussion proceeds.

NOTE.—This is a convenient place to give the etymology of some terms which are frequently used. The word Pædobaptist is made of two Greek words: *paidos*, of a child, and *baptistes*, baptist, and is a name applied to all who practice Infant Baptism. Antipædobaptist means just the opposite to the above, having as a prefix the Greek *anti*, against. The word Anabaptist has the prefix *ana*, anew, and was applied to a sect which arose in Germany in 1522 and held, as close-communion Baptists now hold, that persons baptized in infancy ought to be *baptized anew* on becoming believers.

.

CHAPTER III.

JOHN'S BAPTISM NOT CHRISTIAN BAPTISM.

The only recorded institution of Christian baptism was after Christ's resurrection, when he had finished his personal ministry on earth and was about to ascend his throne. The following is the record of the solemn and memorable occasion:

"Then the eleven disciples went away into Galilee, into a mountain where Jesus had appointed them. And when they saw him, they worshipped him; but some doubted. And Jesus came and spake unto them, saying, *All power is given unto me in heaven and in earth. Go ye therefore, and teach all nations*, BAPTIZING THEM IN THE NAME OF THE FATHER, AND OF THE SON, AND OF THE HOLY GHOST: *Teaching them to observe all things whatsoever I have commanded you: and, lo, I am with you alway, even unto the end of the world.*" (Mat. 28: 16-20.)

Here is the whole of our direct authority for

administering Christian baptism and this our
only Divine warrant to baptize "in the name of
the Father, and of the Son, and of the Holy
Ghost." Here, then, Christian baptism was instituted. It is, indeed, true that the disciples
had before this *baptized;* but there is no evidence that they had done so in the form here
prescribed.

John's baptism was not *Christian* baptism.
Because, First, Christian baptism had not yet
been instituted. The legal dispensation came
to a close only in the death and resurrection of
Christ, after which, as has been seen, Christian
baptism was instituted. The law of Moses
ended in Christ not in John.

Second, John began to baptize six months
before Christ entered upon his public ministry ;
and to suppose that his baptism was Christian
baptism would be to suppose two absurdities,
viz., that the initiatory ordinance of the Christian system existed six months before Chris-
tianity itself, and that Christ did not institute
Christian baptism.

Third, John baptized "with the baptism of
repentance," (Acts 19 : 4), or on profession of

repentance, and not on profession of *regeneration* as in *Christian* baptism.

Fourth, John baptized neither in the name of Christ nor of the Holy Ghost. His disciples afterwards, when interrogated, confessed that they did not know Christ, and that they had " not so much as heard whether there be any Holy Ghost." See Matt. 16: 13, 14, and Acts 19: 2, 3.

Fifth, Paul baptized John's disciples " in the name of the Lord Jesus," (Acts 19: 5,) paying no regard to their having been baptized by John, which he surely would not have done had John's baptism been Christian baptism.

Sixth, That neither John's baptism nor baptism by Christ's disciples before his crucifixion, was Christian baptism is also manifest by the following: John must have baptized very many thousands of people. " Jerusalem and all Judea, and all the region round about Jordan " " went out unto him " and " were *all* baptized of him." And the disciples before Christ's crucifixion baptized great numbers. Yet immediately after Christ's ascension the whole number of the disciples in the New Dispensation was only one hundred and twenty. (Acts 1 : 15.)

Seventh, John's baptism took place under the *Jewish dispensation.* Yet it was not of the law; but was a specific institution for a special purpose, and hence was of only temporary application. The preaching of John and his ministry in general was to "prepare the way of the Lord." His baptism was an ordinance for the time being and was preparatory to the ministry of Christ.

Christ, until his crucifixion, as well as John, recognized the authority of the law of Moses and acted under it. He was "made under the law," circumsized at eight days old, and all his public acts and all that was done in the Church previous to his death, belonged properly to the old dispensation. Hence he submitted to the form of John's baptism "to fulfill all righteousness," that is, to fulfill *every ordinance.*

Eighth, John's baptism was confined to the Jews and was therefore a Jewish ordinance. It was one of those "*divers washings*" mentioned Hebrews 9 : 10, and did not alter Jewish forms of worship, nor did its subjects cease to be members of the Jewish Church on account of their baptism.

Ninth, John's baptism was so called for a purpose. What was that purpose if not to distinguish it from all other baptisms?

Tenth, If John's baptism was the Christian baptism, then its subjects became Christians. As is elsewhere shown, John baptized no less than three millions of Jews. Then the Jewish nation was Christianized before Christ entered upon his ministry and Christ was condemned and crucified by a nation of Christians instead of a nation of Jews, and instead of the number of the disciples after the resurrection being about 120, they were at least 3,000,000. All of which conflicts with Scriptural facts.

The conclusion is, that John's baptism was a Jewish ordinance; its subjects were Jews; and its administrator a Jew, the son of a priest and himself a priest. Could it be shown, as it can not, that John's baptism was by immersion, that would have very little weight in deciding the mode of Christian baptism. And we would not devote a chapter of this book to the consideration of its mode, were it not that immersionists need to be met in that field and defeated there as elsewhere.

CHAPTER IV.

THE MODE OF JOHN'S BAPTISM.

Let us now proceed to investigate the *mode* of John's baptism.

John himself gives us the *mode* of his baptizing, thus, "I indeed baptize you with water unto repentance: but he that cometh after me is mightier than I, whose shoes I am not worthy to bear: he shall baptize you with the Holy Ghost, and with fire." (Matt. 3:11.) We submit to the candid reader that this description, given by the administrator himself, not only does not mean immersion, to the exclusion of every other thought or opinion, as immersionists would have us all believe or else unchurch us all: but that it does not even so much as allow the possibility of immersion.

Let us try the definitions given by the representative immersionists and see if this be true. Take Dr. Carson's definition of *baptize*, "to dip and to dip only," which is accepted by the whole army of immersionists; and Rev. Alexander Campbell's definition of the action as previously quoted: "We must dip, only once, and the motion must be backwards," in which we also understand all immersionists of this day agree with him. Now substitute these two definitions for *baptize*, the term defined by them, and we have John defining the rite performed by himself with water and the work done by Christ with the Holy Ghost and fire, in the following singular, not to say obscure, language: "I indeed dip you, only once, backwards, with water: but he shall dip you, only once, backwards, with the Holy Ghost and with fire." This illustrates the absurdity which results from the unauthorized assumptions and dogmatical assertions of extreme partisans who are blinded by the inflated shadow of only one idea.

The real issue on the subject of the mode of baptism, is, whether the water is to be applied to the subject, or the subject applied to the water. John settles this question, so far as it regards his baptism, by stating that it was "*with* water," that is, the water was applied to the subject.

But, having shown that John's baptism was not the Christian baptism, it follows that the mode of its administration does not determine the question as to the mode of Christian baptism. If it could be proved that John baptized by immersion, that would not prove that Christian baptism should be by immersion. Yet it will not be without interest and profit to the reader for us to investigate the circumstances of John's baptism, so as to see how fully they corroborate his own statement as to the mode.

We do not hesitate to say that the facts and circumstances of John's baptism not only render immersion improbable: but we go further and say that they show immersion to have been impossible. For proof take the following facts:

First. The numbers baptized by John rendered immersion in the case impossible. From Josephus' account of the population of Palestine, A. D. 68, it has been estimated, that it amounted in John's day to not less than *seven millions and a half.* John was commissioned to go to the Jews and he was *unanimously* received by them. There was no division of sentiment in regard to him, as in regard to Christ, and even the Pharisees and Saduces submitted to his baptism. The whole Jewish nation were ambitious of the distinction conferred by his baptism. Hence, " And there went out unto him *all the land of Judea* and they of Jerusalem and were ALL baptized of him in the river of Jordan, confessing their sins." (Mark 1 : 5.) The land of Judea was more than half of the land of Palestine west of the Jordan, and was the most populous part of it. John, therefore, must have baptized not less than *three millions* of people. This number, though very large, is probably below rather than above the correct number; for Matthew says that " Jerusalem, and *all* Judea and *all* the region round about Jordan, went out to him and were baptized," and Mark adds particular emphasis by saying that they " were ALL baptized."

Now it is known that the public ministry of John continued for only about nine months, or two hundred and seventy-five days. It was not lawful for baptism to be performed on Sabbaths, and 40 days must be taken off for these. This would leave 235 days : and probably not all these were occupied in baptizing, as he would not probably begin until by some days of preaching he had convinced the people of his mission, and as his ministry included the winter season, during which there would be in that climate many days of inclement weather on which there would be no traveling about. So that 220 days is a liberal allowance for the number that he could have employed in baptizing.

Now, supposing John to have been a man of the strongest physical endurance, which is not known, six hours a day is as long as he could endure to stand three feet deep in water and baptize for 220 days so nearly in succession, and especially as a part were in the winter season. This would give 1,320 hours in which to baptize 3,000,000 persons. To accomplish this would require that he should baptize at the rate of thirteen thousand six hundred and thirty-eight per day: or two thousand two hundred and eighty-three per hour: or thirty-six per minute: or five in every eight seconds: or one in every second and a half, for six solid hours every day for 220 days in rapid succession.

The veriest tyro can see at once that no hu-

man being could baptize at such rate by immersion. It is simply impossible. And yet the
facts on which the above calculations are made
are Scriptural, and, therefore, cannot be dis-
puted. And who ever claims that John's baptism was by immersion, and on that claim un-
churches forty-nine fiftieths of the whole Christian world, exhibits deplorable ignorance or a
blinded prejudice which is scarcely less pitiable.

These considerations become the more strik-
ing when we consider the facts : first, that much
of the water of the Jordan came from the melt-
ing snows in the mountains about its sources
and was consequently cold, and, secondly, that
the current is remarkably rapid and turbulent.
Robinson, in his Physical Geography of the Holy
Land, page 162, states that the distance from
the Lake of Tiberias to the Dead Sea is sixty-five
miles, and that the difference in the depression
of the two lakes is 666 feet. This marks the
rate of the descent of the Jordan between the
two to be an average of 10.2 feet for each
mile of its direct course. And on page 160
he states that, at the part of the river where
both Latin and Greek traditions locate the Sa-

vior's baptism, "the current is swift, deep and strong," so "very swift and strong, that the stoutest swimmers were carried down many yards in crossing," the width being only about forty yards. The fall of the Mississippi River is only a few inches to the mile.

W. F. Lynch, of the U. S. Navy, who was sent on an exploring expedition to the Jordan in 1847, was compelled to use metallic boats in descending it. In his journal he states that he found the current "about twelve miles an hour," "one foaming rapid," "with its tumultuous rush the river hurried us onward, and we knew not what the next moment would bring forth." "Sometimes, placing our sole trust in Providence, we plunged with headlong velocity down appalling descents:" "a camel in the river, washed down by the current in attempting to cross the ford last night." And even at the spot where tradition locates the baptism of Christ by John, he found the current so impetuous that while some bathed, the boats were placed a little below "to be in readiness to render assistance should any of the crowd be swept down by the current, and in

danger of drowning." Indeed so dangerous was
the river at this point, though not more so than
elsewhere, that Lieut. Lynch, laboring under
the delusion that Christ was immersed, was
compelled to imagine a miracle to render his
baptism possible. His language is, "On that
wondrous day, when the Deity, veiled in flesh,
descended the bank, all nature, hushed in awe,
looked on; and the impetuous river, in grateful
homage, must have stayed its course and gently
laved the body of its Lord." Expedition to
the Dead Sea and the Jordan, pages 256-266.

Now any one can see that no human being
could have stood in this cold and dangerous
current six hours a day for 220 days, even if it
were not otherwise impossible, as previously
shown, for John to have immersed the immense multitudes whom he baptized. Immersion in the case is clearly a physical impossibility.

If any ask, by what mode, then, John could
have baptized so many in the time specified,
we answer: He himself tells us that he was not
sent to abolish the Jewish rites, nor to introduce new ones; but to observe them. Had he

undertaken to abolish the old or to introduce new ones, he would have met with opposition from the Jews instead of being unanimously received by them. The Jews had a custom of figuratively purifying the people by dipping a branch of hyssop in water and sprinkling it upon them. We are told, Heb. 9 : 19, that Moses took the blood of calves and of goats and with hyssop sprinkled all the people. It is, therefore, probable that John, in baptizing the people with water, did not depart from the Jewish custom ; but followed the usage of Moses, and sprinkled the people in great numbers as they came to him, with a bunch of hyssop made sufficiently large for his purpose. This was the Jewish mode of purification, which Paul calls baptism.

If it is supposed that our estimate of the numbers which John baptized is too high, we will state for the benefit of any who so think, that according to·the lowest estimate we have seen, and supposing that only one-third instead of "*all*" the people named by Matthew and Mark, came out to him and were baptized, even in that case it would have taken John three years and a half to have immersed them, instead of nine months, supposing that he had immersed one person every two minutes and continued in the water ten hours every day.

Second. But another and very serious difficulty is in the way of allowing that John's baptism was by immersion, viz: Were these meriads immersed in a state of nudity, in baptismal robes, or in their clothes? In the first condition would have been an outrage and is not a possible supposition. Baptismal robes were unheard of until centuries afterwards. Then they must have been immersed in their wearing apparel and returned dripping to their respective homes: for even if it could be supposed that so great a multitude had gone out provided with a change of clothing, to have made the change under the circumstances would have been an outrage. Now, what is to be said of the likeliness of such a spectacle in the name of religion and on the score of health and decency? And this question becomes the more forcible when it is considered that multitudes of these people were many miles distant from their homes, as any can see by consulting a map of Palestine.

Added to these reflections, the reader may

consider the presumption against immersion
contained in the fact that the Scripture nowhere makes any mention of a changing or lay-
ing aside of garments in connection with the
performance of baptism.   This fact is the more
noticeable when it is considered that mention
is made of garments, where there could be no
more necessity nor propriety of mentioning
them, than in the case of baptism, supposing
baptism to have been performed by immersion.
For instance: When our Lord washed his disciples' feet, it is said, "he laid aside his garments." (John 12:4.)   And Luke, speaking of
the stoning of Stephen, says: "The witnesses
laid down their clothes at a young man's feet,
whose name was Saul." (Acts 7:58.)

Now, if the Scriptures notice the apparently
unimportant fact of the putting off of garments
in such cases as the above-mentioned, how
comes it to pass that no hint is dropped of a
change or putting off of garments in any of the
numerous cases of baptism? It can be ac-
counted for only on- the supposition that no
such putting off of garments took place.   And
this is strong presumptive evidence against im-

mersion. Think of the multitudes who flocked
to John's preaching, and were baptized, doubtless, without having anticipated or prepared for
it: the baptism of Christ; and the baptism of
the eunuch, where evidently neither Philip nor
the eunuch had expected or prepared for it;
and suppose immersion in all these cases and
not a hint about garments! And the same remarkable omission may be mentioned in the
other baptisms recorded in the New Testament,
especially the baptism of Paul, of the three
thousand, of the jailor, of Cornelius and his
friends and of the sundry household baptisms.

Third. In speaking of John's baptism, the
administrator himself and Luke, who was a
physician and scholar, use the Dative, without
a preposition, to express the manner of it
Greek scholars will understand this as
"the Dative of the instrument." The Dative
case, when thus used, means "the instrument
with which a thing is accomplished" (Anthon's
Grammar). "I indeed baptize you—*hudati*—
with water." (Luke 3 : 16.) "John indeed
baptized—*hudati—with water.*" (Acts 1 : 5.)
"Then remembered I the word of the Lord,

how that he said, John indeed baptized—*hudati* —*with water.*,' (Acts 11 : 16.)

The use of the "Dative of the instrument," it being without a preposition, precludes the possibility of John's baptism being *in* water. It was *with* water, as the instrument. The water was applied to the subject, and not the subject to the water. If I say "I struck a horse *with* a whip," the whip is *the instrument* and is applied to the horse, and not the horse to the whip, nor is the horse put in the whip. Matthew, in recording the same sentence as Luke 3 : 16, "I indeed baptize you with water," uses *en hudati* to express "with water" instead of *hudati*, the Dative of the instrument, as used by Luke, and the Greek preposition *en* is frequently thus used with the Dative case of the noun as synonimous with the Dative of the instrument. See Matt. 23 : 37, "*En, with* all thy heart, and, *en, with* all thy soul, and, *en, with* all thy mind." Also see Luke 14 : 34 and Matt. 6 : 29.

Fourth. Immersionists say that John's baptism was performed *in the Jordan* and, therefore, must have been immersion. "Were baptized of him in Jordan," Matt. 3:6; "And were all baptized of him in the river of Jordan," Mark 1:5. If the expression "in the river of Jordan" above proves immersion, as is so confidently claimed, then we will ask the one who thus claims to tell us what the similar expressions in the following prove? " John did baptize in the wilderness," Mark 1:4; "These things were done in Bethabara, beyond Jordan, where John was baptizing," John 1:28. If the fact that he baptized "in the Jordan" proves beyond question that it was done by immersion, the fact that he baptized "in the wilderness" and "in Bethabara, *beyond* Jordan," proves, we should think, beyond question, that it was not done by immersion. The same Greek preposition, *en*, is used in all three cases. Thus the "in Jordan" argument is, to say the least, doubly offset.

But can these apparently conflicting statements be reconciled? Easily; if one will lay aside his preconceived prejudices and view the case with common sense in the light of facts. Biblical geography teaches us that the Jordan has double banks. In the inner banks, about

I

forty yards wide, the water flows at ordinary
stages.   In the outer banks, about a quarter of
a mile wide, it flows in freshets.   It was cus-
tomary to say of whatever was done inside of
these outer banks, that it was done " in the
Jordan."   See 2 Kings 6:4: " And when they
came (*eis ton Iordanan*—Septuagint) to (should
be *into*) Jordan they cut down wood."   Here
the Greek preposition, *eis*, is put after the verb
of motion and before the Accusative of the object, which, as Greek scholars know, is the
strongest form of the language to express *into* a
place, and in this instance locates these beam-
choppers and house-builders — see 2 Kings
6:2—"in the Jordan " while "cutting down
wood."   Of course inside the outer banks of
the Jordan, or in the valley of the Jordan, is
meant.   Thus it may easily be seen how it is
true that John baptized "in Jordan," "in the
wilderness " and "beyond Jordan " as well.
When viewed in the light of the truth that he
sprinkled the people when he baptized them,
there is no confliction in the statements.   But
claim that he immersed the people and then
try to reconcile these statements and you will

at once find yourself involved in trouble. Truly, as Mr. Miller has pertinently said, "The valley of Jordan is a land of sorrow for immersionists."

The Septuagint or Alexandrine version, from which the above quotation from 2 Kings is taken, is a translation of the Old Testament from the Hebrew language to the Greek, made 150 to 275 years before Christ. Of its authority and accuracy, we need say nothing in addition to the statement that Christ and the apostles, in referring to the Old Testament, quoted from this version.

Fifth. It is urged in support of immersion that "John baptized in Enon, near to Salim, because there was much water there," John 3 : 23. It is argued that John chose a place where there was "much water" for the reason that water was needed for immersing the people. This argument loses the whole of its force by one stroke when it is remembered that John went to Enon, the place of "much water," from the banks of the Jordan, a place of more water than Enon. The Jordan, as heretofore shown, is a deep river forty feet wide; if Enon was a place of any body of water large enough for immersion it has to this date eluded the search of travelers and explorers. At any rate if the motive for selecting Enon was in order to have *much water* for immersing, we are left to wonder why he left the place of *more* water for the place of less water. Let any one explain who can.

The true reason for the removal from the Jordan to Enon was doubtless as follows: Enon is a term of Hebrew origin and means *a spring* or *springs.* The Greek words "*polla hudata*," which are translated "much water," being in the plural number, would be more naturally translated "many waters." When the same writer uses these same words elsewhere, they are so translated. See Rev. 1 : 15, "And his voice as the sound of *many waters.*"

Therefore Enon was a locality where there were either a number of springs, or small streams flowing from a spring. The water was good for drinking and clothes-washing purposes. The Jordan was a rapid and turbulent river and its waters muddy and dark and not fit for drinking until after standing many hours.

Especially was this the case in the winter and spring, the seasons during which John was baptizing. When the immense multitudes flocked to his baptism, as elsewhere shown, it is easy to see why John would move from the Jordan to Enon. The intention to immerse, if such had existed, would have led him to remain at the Jordan.

As a suitable offset to the " much water " argument of Immersionists, we give the following from The Pædobaptist's Guide, by the recent John Guthrie, D.D., of Scotland :

"We grudge to spend more time over this most frivolous of arguments; but we cannot dismiss it without observing, that this "much water" argument is a two-edged weapon, which might be turned against its propounders with very damaging effect. If "much water" make for them, little water will make against them. How comes it, then, that of the nine or ten places mentioned in the New Testament, where baptisms were performed, only two—namely, Ænon and Jordan—had "much water?" How comes it that in some of these places there was but little water, and that, too, as we shall yet see, when thousands upon thousands were to be baptized? As Professor Wilson, of Belfast, well puts this argument: '*Much* water is the exception, *little* water the rule. The ordinance could, indeed, be administered in the river Jordan, and at the many streams of Ænon; but so simple was the rite, that its performance appears to have been equally convenient in a private house, a prison, or a desert. If, then, the volume of the Jordan is requisite to pour vigor into the Baptist argument for immersion, how sapless and feeble must that argument become when its nutriment is drawn from the stinted supply of a prison, or the thirsty soil of a wilderness.' Thus, the 'much water' argument fatally rebounds. It is a reed powerful only to pierce the hand that leans upon it."

We now ask the thoughtful reader whether or not he has found any immersion in the "*in Jordan*" and "*much water*" arguments of Immersionists, and remark that these are all the reasons which they can claim for their bold assertions about John's baptism. In the language of Mr. Hibbard, if, after all these facts, any one "be not satisfied of the improbability and impossibility of the immersion theory, we must, perhaps, leave him in the undisturbed and everlasting repose of his chosen, yet baseless faith."

CHAPTER V.

CHRIST'S BAPTISM.

The inexperienced and less informed are frequently pressed to follow the example of Christ in baptism, it being first assumed that he was immersed and that his baptism was intended to be an example for Christians. Perhaps no other appeal is used with half the effect of this upon those who have not informed themselves as to facts about Christ's baptism.

We ask the reader's careful attention to the following:

First. The baptism of Christ did not partake of the character of John's baptism. Because: 1. John's baptism was "the baptism of repentance," otherwise said to be "unto repentance," or in testimony of their repentance. To suppose that the baptism of Christ was "the baptism of repentance," in testimony of his repentance of sin, would be blasphemy. 2. Doubtless the formula used in John's baptism

is given by Paul in the following: " John verily
baptized with the baptism of repentance, saying
unto the people that they should believe on
him who should come after him, that is, on
Christ Jesus," Acts 19:4. If, therefore, this
was the baptism received by Christ, John must
have exhorted him to the faith of *a Messiah to
come* and Christ must have accepted that faith.
Which is absurd.   3. The design of John's
baptism was to "prepare the way of the Lord,"
or to prepare the hearts of the people to receive
Christ.   But this import of baptism could not
apply to the Savior in any way.

Second.   Nor did the baptism of Christ par-
take· of the character of Christian baptism.
Because: 1. As has been shown in Chapter
III, Christian baptism was not instituted until
after Christ's resurrection, three years after his
baptism.   Its first administration was on the day
of Pentecost.   2. Christian baptism is in the
name of the Holy Trinity, the candidate there-
by testifying his faith in the existence and glory
of Father, Son and Holy Ghost.   It is absurd
to suppose Christ being baptized in his own
name and professing faith in and devotion to

his own cause. 3. Christian baptism is both a
sign and a *seal* in its *import.* As a *sign* it witnesses the inward washing or regeneration,
which presupposes defilement by sin. As a
seal it is a pledge of our fidelity to God and
of his fidelity to us. Can any one suppose this
sign and *seal* applicable to Christ?

Third. Christ's baptism was not for the purpose of furnishing an example for Christians.
Because : 1. There are two New Testament
Sacraments, the Lord's Supper and Baptism.
If Christ's example was important in one it was
in the other. But we know that Christ did not
participate in the elements of the eucharist; but
only gave to his disciples. See Matt. 26 : 27-29.
If he left no example of personal celebration of
the eucharist, is it not a strong presumption
that he left none as to baptism? 2. Christ
was thirty years old when he was baptized. Is
it a suitable example for young Christians to
defer baptism until that age ; or does such delay comport with the early piety of Christ? To
suppose his baptism an example for his follow-
ers would be to suppose it an example of *pro-
crastinaton !* 3. The evangelists relate the bap-

tism of the people as taking place previous to Christ's: "Now when all the people were baptized, it came to pass that Jesus also, being baptized," etc., Luke 3 : 21. See also Matthew and Mark. If it were Christ's purpose to set an example for others to follow, it is strange that he should wait until thousands, not to say millions, had been baptized previous to him. 4. It is not written in the Scripture that Christ was baptized to set an example for Christians to follow, nor is such doctrine deducible from the sacred text.

We conclude, therefore, that the vigorous and often-repeated appeals to the pious sensibilities of young disciples to "follow the example of Christ" in baptism, is vain and gratuitous babbling, and has the appearance of being an effort of the unscrupulous to take advantage of the unwary.

The reader will ask, Why then was the baptism of Christ necessary, or what was its purpose? The answer is at hand. Christ himself furnishes it. When John declined to baptize him, saying, "I have need to be baptized of thee, and comest thou to me," the Savior answered: "Suffer it to be so now; for thus it becometh us to fulfill all righteousness," Matt. 3:14, 15. This answer satisfied John and he proceeded with the baptism. "To fulfill all righteousness" was, therefore, Christ's language to express the necessity and purpose of his baptism. What then does this language mean?

The phrases to "fulfill all righteousness," to "fulfill the righteousness of the law" and to "fulfill the law," are used in the New Testament with similar import and refer to the fulfillment of the Mosaic law. When the Savior said to the Jews, "Think not that I am come to destroy the law or the prophets: I am not come to destroy, but to fulfill," Matt. 5:17, he evidently referred to the fulfillment of the Mosaic law and the form of speech is identical with that used by him to express the necessity and purpose of his baptism. Other instances might be given to show that the fulfillment of the requirements of the Mosaic law was what Christ meant by *fulfilling all righteousness*, but it is deemed unnecessary here.

At the time of his baptism Christ was about to enter upon his public ministry. He had reached his thirtieth year—the age at which, under the Mosaic code, the priests were to enter upon the duties of their office and to receive their priestly consecration. Christ was a "high priest" and exercised the functions of a priest when he purged the temple, and when on that occasion his authority was demanded, he appealed to the baptism of John as giving him, according to the law and custom, the authority of a priest. And if we search the whole Mosaic code we will find no law requiring Christ's baptism at the particular time it took place, except the one regulating priestly consecration.

Much of the argument and arrangement of what has gone before in this chapter, is from the excellent book of Rev. F. G. Hibbard on Christian Baptism, a book of near 600 pages, which we cordially recommend to our readers. We now give the reader the benefit of the following quotation from "Baptism Tested by Scripture and History," by Rev. Wm. Hodges, Covington, Ky.:

"Until his crucifixion, Christ, as well as John, acted under and recognized the authority of the law of Moses; he was circumcised on the eighth day, brought to the temple and presented to the Lord, after his mother's purification; attended the public worship of the temple, and drove from its hallowed courts the money changers, who would change his Father's house of prayer into a den of thieves. When he cleansed a leper, he bid him "go and show thyself unto the priest, and offer for thy cleansing, according as Moses commanded, for a testimony unto them," (Luke 5 : 14.) And in his *public* teaching to the multitude, told them, " The scribes and pharisees sit in Moses' seat: All, therefore, whatsoever they bid you observe, that observe and do; but do not ye after their works; for they say and do not." (Matt. 23 : 2, 3.) Almost the last thing that he did before he suffered, was in obedience to Moses, to observe the "passover.' (Matt. 26 : 17-25.) But here ended the Old Dispensation.

" He had united with John in preparing the people for the New. He had submitted to his baptism, not because he needed repentance, but as recognizing John's mission and appointment from Heaven, and his ritual purification for the introduction of the New Dispensation, and as submitting himself also to all Heaven's regulations 'under the law'—'to fulfill all righteousness.' (Matt. 3 : 15.) And it may be, to set him apart for his priestly office, as was Aaron.

For John's baptism, as a preparation for the Gospel of Christ, was certainly very similar to the purification of the Israelites, to prepare them for the reception of the law at Mount Sinai. (See Exodus 19.)"

We, therefore, conclude that the *necessity* for Christ's baptism existed in the fact that he needed to be consecrated to the priestly office and that baptism did that,—Ex. 29 and Lev. 7. And that this consecration or setting apart to the priestly office was of manifest necessity in his case, we need not take space to argue, but will only suggest, as an illustration, that this consecration was needed in order to vindicate his authority as a priest on such occasions as the purging of the temple, heretofore referred to.

We conclude also, that the *purpose* of Christ's baptism was to vindicate the majesty and to magnify the import of the "law and the prophets" by his compliance, who was himself the "end of the law"—to whom all the types and prophesies pointed and in whom they met—who was himself the "high priest" in whose character God was to illustrate that justice in whose unbalanced scales man had been found wanting and to exhibit his infinite love to man.

The man who, in the light of the above facts, drawn from the sacred oracles, will still persist in urging the uninformed to follow the example of Christ in "fulfilling all righteousness" by immersion in "the liquid grave," is an object of commiseration.

We will now proceed to consider the question of the mode of Christ's baptism. This we do, not because we think the mode of it, whatever it was, established the proper mode of Christian baptism, but because, as previously stated, we wish to meet and defeat Immersionists in every part of the field.

First. Having shown that Christ's baptism was his consecration to the priest's office, it remains to inquire by what mode do the Scriptures inform us the water was used in such consecration. In the case of Aaron and his sons the record of consecration is, "And Aaron and his sons thou shalt bring to the door of the tabernacle of the congregation, and shalt wash them with water," Ex. 29:4. In this case the *action* was *with* water. But the whole tribe of

Levi were to be consecrated to the service of the sanctuary, as well as Aaron and his sons. And that which is expressed in general terms, in the case of the latter, viz: "Thou shalt wash them with water," is in the case of the consecration of the Levites given in specific and particular terms as to its manner. "And thus shalt thou do unto them to cleanse them: sprinkle water of purification upon them." Here the mode of applying the water in the consecration is established by Divine appointment. Now, as the Scriptures are as silent as the grave as to any change of this Divine law and long-prevailing custom, in the case of the baptism or consecration of Christ, we are forced to the conclusion that no such change took place and that Christ fulfilled the law in this particular, as in all others.

Second. The reliance to prove that Christ's baptism was by immersion is the use of the prepositions *in* and *out of* in the record: "And was baptized of John in Jordan. And straightway coming out of the water," etc., Mark 1: 9, 10. On this we make the following remarks:

That the Greek preposition *eis*, which, in this

case, is translated "in," and the Greek preposition *apo*, which is translated "out of," are much more frequently translated *to, at, by, with*, etc., and *from*. Prepositions of similar import are used in the case of the baptism of the eunuch, where *eis* is translated "into," and *ek* "out of." In these two instances, viz: the baptism of Christ and the baptism of the eunuch, our translators were partial to the Immersionists; for the *en* and *eis*, which they here render "*in*" and "*into*"— as "into the water," they have rendered *to* or *unto* in 538 cases: *apo*, which they here render "out of"—as "out of the water," they have in 374 cases rendered *from*; and *ek*, which is here rendered "out of," is in 186 other instances rendered *from*. Thus it is readily seen that the *in-the-Jordan* and *out-of-the-water* argument is offset hundreds of fold and that the prepositions used in them, when intelligently weighed in the light of facts, turn upon the Immersionists who wield them with crushing power, like the elephants of King Pyrrhus' army.

And it is quite as apparent that Mark's record of Christ's baptism, as above quoted, may be with equal or greater correctness rendered thus: "And was baptized of John *at* the Jordan. And straightway coming up *from* the water," etc. And New Testament usage determines that it should neither be "*in*" nor "*into*," but "*at* the Jordan:" and that it should not be "*out of*," but "*from* the water." Our Immersionist friends are well enough pleased with King James' translators as long as the version favors their pet and partisan views, but are irreconcilably opposed when any term is so rendered as not to prop up the visionary idea of immersion as a substitute for Christian baptism.

Third.   We have shown in the previous chapter that the expression "in the Jordan," which, it is freely conceded, is *a* correct rendering of the original Greek, but not *the only* correct one, did not mean necessarily in the water of the Jordan, but rather in the valley of the Jordan. In addition to what is there said, we will here say, that the reader will more readily apprehend and appreciate this fact if he will examine the map of the Jordan and its valley, which accompanies Lieut. Lynch's "Exploration of the Jordan and the Dead Sea." When the Savior came from Galilee to John to be baptized, he found him "in the Jordan" baptizing, in the the same way that the choppers were "in the Jordan cutting down wood," mentioned in the previous chapter. That is, in the valley, or within the outer banks of the Jordan, or "in the wilderness" in the valley of the river: all of which are expressions which mean the same thing. This will be the more readily accepted as true when it is remembered that immediately following his baptism " he was *there in the wilderness* forty days, tempted of the devil." Mark 1 : 13.

The same phrase in the Greek which would put Christ *in the water* of the river Jordan receiving baptism, and John and his numberless disciples *in the water* of the same river and Philip and the eunuch *in the water*, and all for the pleasure of enthusiastic but over credulous Immersionists, would also locate "the sons of the prophets" in the midst of the rapid current and the waves of the deep and turbulent waters of the Jordan while "cutting down wood" and "felling beams." 2 Kings 6: 4, 5. And the same Greek word and the same reasoning which locate John and Christ *in the water* of the Jordan for baptism, present Christ as taking up his abode *in the water* of that dangerous stream, viz: Jesus went "into the place where John at first baptized; and there he abode." John 10: 40.

When an argument proves too much it proves nothing and is even worse, it becomes repulsive to him who wields it; and one would think that the above facts would render the "in-the-Jordan" argument, which is the only one they have, as repulsive to Immersionists as was the magic balsam of Sanco Panza to the credulous and disappointed stomach of Don Quixote.

Fourth. Granting that Christ was really *in the water* of the river of Jordan, does that prove so clearly that he was immersed, as to justify the one-fiftieth part of the Christian world, who so believe, in unchurching the other forty-nine fiftieths who do not so believe? We think not, for these reasons: The Oriental costume, when girt up, left the feet uncovered except by soles, which were easily slipped off and on, so that to be standing in the water would be no discomfort, but rather the opposite, especially in a warm and dry climate. Indeed, we know of no valid objection to supposing that John stood

upon the bank of the river, as the Christian art
of the fourth and fifth centuries represents him
in pictures, frequently dipping his bunch of hyssop into the water and with it sprinkling the
willing thousands—publicans and soldiers as
well, Luke 3 : 12-14—who would pass in crowds
in the edge of the river before him. This supposition can be the more readily considered
from the fact that they would thus gain the
cooling and refreshing effects of the water on
their lower extremities and would avoid the
dust which would, under other circumstances,
attend the presence and moving of such multitudes. The earliest Christian art, in numerous
pictures which are still in existence, represents
John standing upon the bank of the Jordan and
Christ standing in the water before him, while
he is receiving baptism by affusion. These pictures by the early Christians show how they
understood that Christ's baptism was performed.
There being *nothing*, ABSOLUTELY NOTHING, to
the contrary, I, for one, am willing to accept
the teachings of these early Christians on this
subject, seeing they agree with Scripture.

Dr. Thompson, the missionary, describes the

Jordan pilgrims of the present age as plunging
into the river and there performing acts of cer-
emonial purification by standing and pouring
water on each other's heads, in imitation of the
baptism of Christ. And Lieut. Lynch, in his
book heretofore mentioned, describes the very
spot in the Jordan where tradition locates the
baptism of Christ and, although he seems to
have accepted, we suppose without investiga-
tion, the mythical idea that said baptism was
by immersion, he gives us an engraving of the
scene of some of these enthusiastic pilgrims
performing these purifications, while two of his
metallic boats, well manned, are placed below
to save any who might be in danger of drowning from the force and rapidity of the current.

I again quote from Dr. Guthrie:

"Where, then, I ask, is there the slightest
trace that the blessed Savior was immersed?
On this point the prepositions are silent; 'baptizo' is silent; and if the Evangelists otherwise
are silent, where is this much vaunted case of
immersion? There being no evidence that our
Lord was immersed, we conclude that he was
baptized by sprinkling or pouring. For, (1.)
That was the mode in the Jewish 'purifications,'

which were just so many 'baptisms,' to the entire exclusion of immersion. (2.) All the pro-
prieties of the case, before noticed, militate here
with augmented force against the idea of immersion. (3.) The manner in which the Spirit
descended on the Savior's head harmonizes best
with the mode by pouring, and with the universal tenor of inspired language, both in the Old
Testament and the New, which represents the
Spirit as 'poured out' or 'falling upon' us, and
not as dipped or plunged into the Spirit."

CHAPTER VI.

CHRISTIAN BAPTISM.

We have shown on page 15, that Christian baptism was instituted after the resurrection of Christ and that its history is after that event. There are nine cases of Christian baptism recorded in the New Testament. So far as the history of the ordinance is concerned these nine administrations are the only sources from which we can draw information. If, from the circumstances attending them, we can determine the mode of administering, then the question of *mode* is settled for all Christians. If the mode cannot be certainly determined from them, then that mode which appears most probably to have been the one practised in these cases, should have precedence, of course.

We will, therefore, now proceed to investigate these cases and see whether or not the circumstances attending them indicate that the baptized were immersed. We respectfully ask

the reader to enter with us upon this fair inves-
tigation with a mind not preoccupied by opinions and prejudices.

THE THREE THOUSAND.

The first account of the administration of
Christian baptism is in these words: "They
that gladly received his word were baptized,
and the same day there were added unto them
about three thousand souls," Acts 2:41. This
occurred in the city of Jerusalem, on the day of
Pentecost. The principal preacher was Peter;
the audience was composed of citizens and
great numbers who had assembled at Jerusalem
from eighteen or more foreign countries (see
verses 9-11); the administrators were Peter and
the eleven other apostles (see verse 14). Was
this baptism performed by immersion? We
answer, no; for the following reasons:

First. There is not a hint in the Scriptural
narrative which gives the remotest ground on
which to suppose it was immersion. It appears
from the narrative that they were baptized at
the very spot and at the very time that they
believed. On the supposition that these three

thousand subjects were dispersed throughout
and around the city, for the purpose of finding
pools or streams suitable for immersion, the
narrative, to say the least, is an unnatural and
unsatisfactory one. But on the supposition that
the baptism was by sprinkling, the narrative is
natural, easy and satisfactory.

Second. Isaiah, in predicting the humilia-
tion and exaltation of Christ, and the success
which should attend his cause, prophesied that
"many nations" should be introduced into the
Church. (Isaiah 52:7-15.) This prophecy began to be fulfilled on the day of Pentecost, only
a few days after the Savior's ascension, when
the representatives of nineteen or twenty different nations were present to hear, many of them
the first time, the preaching of the gospel and
to witness the outpouring of the Spirit on that
remarkable occasion. In fulfillment of the
prophecy, about three thousand of them were
introduced into the Church by baptism. How
was this baptism performed? Turn back to the
prophecy and read: "So shall he sprinkle many
nations." Isaiah 52:15. Read the fifty-second
chapter of Isaiah and it will occur to you that

the whole scene there predicted was to take place at the very opening of the gospel dispensation: and how completely is it fulfilled in the scene on the day of Pentecost! And who will say that of all the details of the fulfillment, the mode of administration of baptism was the only exception, and yet no allusion in the narrative to such exception and no hint to justify the supposition that it existed?

Third. There was no place nor places for the immersion of so great a multitude on that "same day." The Jordan was twenty-five miles distant. The brook Kidron was an unimportant and turbid stream, which flowed along the east side of the city and the authorities say its channel was always dry, except in winter: and the Pentecost was in June. And if it had not been dry a sewer poured all the filth of the northern part of the city into it, rendering it totally unfit for a place of immersing. Siloam was at the foot of Mount Moriah, three-quarters of a mile from where the apostles were preaching, and we have no account of their going to it with the thousands who heard them: Bethesda was in the control of the priests, the avowed enemies

of the cause of Christ, who ridiculed the trans-
actions of the day, saying: "These men are full
of new wine," and it cannot be supposed that
they would allow its use to the apostles.   For
the same reason, and others, they would not be
allowed the use of the washing lavers of the
temple.   And it cannot be supposed that they
would be admitted in such large numbers to the
few private tanks and cisterns of the rich, for
very few of them were disposed to befriend the
cause of Christ.

Wm. C. Prime, a recent explorer, writes in his
book thus of Jerusalem: "The city is depend-
ent for its supply of water chiefly on the rains
of heaven.   This subject has been a fruitful
source of discussion to Oriental travelers, and
it is very certain that as yet little progress has
been made in explaining where the immense
population that once inhabited Jerusalem ob-
tained their supply of this necessary of life."
The three or four pools which exist in the city,
are stated, on the best authority, to be from
eighteen to forty feet deep and the sides perpendicular, not sloping, so that each one is as
deep at the edge as at any other point.   If the

apostles could have had free access to them, which was impossible, they would still have found immersion impossible, as the most shallow of these pools is eighteen feet perpendicular at the edge.

Fourth. The time allowed for baptizing these three thousand was not sufficient to admit of the supposition that they were immersed. Peter's sermon began at nine o'clock in the morning, "the third hour of the day." Acts 2 : 15. There is no mention of a change of the day until chapter 4, verse 3. All that is narrated from chapter 2 to chapter 4 took place on the day of of Pentecost. At "the ninth hour," or three o'clock P. M., we find Peter and John going quietly into the temple, it being the "hour of prayer." Acts 3 : 1. The preaching, conversions and baptizings all took place in just six hours—from nine A. M. to three P. M. This would give to each one of the twelve apostles six hours for completing the whole of the preaching, instruction and preparation necessary to the conversion of two hundred and fifty persons, mostly foreigners or heathen, and to their baptism. And this all so entirely completed in the given time that Peter and John, two of the *immersionists*, had dried their clothes and were ready to go into the temple to prayer at three in the afternoon!

However the above may be, certainly after the close of Peter's sermon, only a part of the day remained. The converts must be selected from the multitude and questioned as to their faith and experience. And, as they had come together with no expectation of conversion nor baptism, if immersed, they were to be provided with a change of raiment, etc., etc. All this would occasion great delay. Now, suppose the apostles had access to even all the places above mentioned, it was impossible for twelve administrators to have scattered about to these distant, inconvenient and inadequate places and to have immersed three thousand in so limited a time. And this is the more palpable when it is considered that the administrators and their three thousand subjects were all alike taken by surprise by the circumstances of the occasion. Not having anticipated the scenes they had not prepared for them. But no such difficulties exist on the supposition that the baptism was

performed according to the prophecy, by sprinkling, the prevalent mode of purifying among
the Jews.

We again quote from Mr. Miller's admirable
little book:

"The very men who would fain believe, in
the face of all these facts, that these three thousand were immersed would, as a jury, hang a
man until he was dead, dead, upon as strong
evidence that he had committed murder as the
above is against their dogma."

CHAPTER VII.

CHRISTIAN BAPTISM—THE SAMARITANS.

The second case of Christian baptism on record was by Philip in Samaria of quite a number of the population: "But when they believed Philip preaching the things concerning the kingdom of God, and the name of Jesus Christ, they were baptized, both men and women." Acts 8 : 12. There are no circumstances in this case which indicade the mode, except that it appears that they were baptized at the very time when and on the very spot where they believed. And this is a suitable place to remark, that this circumstance is uniform in the cases of Christian baptism in the New Testament. There is nowhere any mention of going away to or in search of a stream or pool, nor of any arrangement or delay to prepare for a change of garments, but immediately upon believing and at the very spot, the subjects were baptized. Is it likely that such would have been the uniform record had the various cases of baptism been by immersion?

THE EUNUCH.

The third case of Christian baptism is that of the Ethiopean eunuch by Philip, recorded in the eighth chapter of Acts. Immersionists say that the circumstances of this case prove immersion beyond dispute, but an intelligent examination of the case shows that its circumstances are conclusive in favor of sprinkling. We ask the reader to turn to Acts 8 : 26-39, and read the history of the case and thus he will be the better prepared to consider the circumstances with us.

As will be seen, this eunuch was a man of high authority and power and had charge of all the treasures of the queen of Ethiopia. He was a Jew and had gone up to Jerusalem in his chariot to worship, as a Jew, not as a Christian. On his return, having in his possession a copy of the Jewish Scriptures, he was leisurely reading, while pursuing his journey, that wonderful prophecy of Christ which begins at Isaiah 52 : 13, and continues through Isaiah 53. The reader will bear in mind that at that time the Scriptures had not been divided into chapters.

Philip, just from the scenes of his preaching and baptizing in Samaria, was directed by the Spirit, so that he met the eunuch on the highway, just at the time that he was reading this prophecy, and, accosting him, he said: "Understandest thou what thou readest?" In reply the eunuch confessed that he did not understand and could not without a teacher. Having invited Philip to sit with him in the chariot, he inquired of him whether the prophet wrote those wonderful predictions "of himself or of some other." Immediately Philip "began at the same Scripture, and preached unto him Jesus." The eunuch was convinced and believed; and as they proceeded on their way, seeing water, he proposed that he receive baptism, which Philip at once administered on his earnest profession of faith. Now, the question is, was this baptism performed by immersion? We say it was not, for the following and other reasons :

First. The sole ground upon which it can be claimed that this was an immersion, is the expression that they both "went down into the water" and came "up out of the water." The

Greek prepositions *eis* and *ek*, which are here translated "*into*" and "*out of*," are, in hundreds of other cases, as previously intimated, translated "*to*" and "*from;*" and are in very many instances used where their translation by "into" and "out of" is impossible. The expression then would be more in conformity to the original if translated "went down *to* the water" and came "up *from* the water." Of this we will say more as we proceed. That the translators rendered it as they did, we can account for only on the supposition that they were themselves inclined to the immersion theory, which we have also other reasons for thinking was the case. Let the reader now for a moment reflect on the absurdity of deciding an important question, which is made to determine as to the ecclesiastical order and to test the spirit of obedience or disobedience of Christendom, on the simple question as to the correctness or incorrectness of the translation of two Greek prepositions, in any particular place, which are otherwise and variously translated in other places in Scripture!

Second. The Greek particle *eis*, which is

here rendered *into*, is used with other significa-
tions in very many places in Scripture; some of
which are here given as samples: "Go thou *to*
(*eis*) the sea,"—not *into* the sea.   Matt. 17: 27.
"I am not sent but *unto* (*eis*) the lost sheep of
the house of Israel,"—not *into* the lost sheep.
Matt. 15 : 24.   "Come *unto* (*eis*) the marriage,"
—not *into* the marriage.   The Evangelist John
declares positively that in the following passage
eis does not mean *into:* "Peter therefore went
forth, and that other disciple, and came *to* (*eis*)
the sepulchre. * * And the other disciple did
outrun Peter, and came first *to* (*eis*) the sepulchre:
* * *yet went he not in.*"   John 20: 3-5.   Examples might be multiplied almost indefinitely, as
eis is rendered *to* or *unto* 538 times; but certainly
these are sufficient to show that *eis* would take
Philip and the eunuch *to* the water; but no
further.

Also, the Greek preposition *ek*, which is here
translated "out of," is otherwise used as follows: "Sever the wicked *from* (*ek*) the just,"—
certainly not *out of* the just.   Matt. 13:49.
"The tree is known *by* (*ek*) its fruits,"—certainly not *out of* its fruits.   Matt. 12:23.   "Many

good works have I shown you *from* (*ek*) my father,"—surely not *out of* my father. "And he riseth *from* (*ek*) supper, and laid aside his garments,"—not *out of* supper. "When he shall return *from* (*ek*) the wedding." "And they shall gather together his elect *from* (*ek*) the four winds." As in the case of *eis*, examples might be multiplied indefinitely, as *ek* is rendered *from* 186 times; but the above are enough to show that *ek* would bring Philip and the eunuch *from* the water only.

It is therefore evident that the language used in reference to Philip and the eunuch can prove nothing more than that they descended from their seats in the chariot to the water and that after the baptism they ascended again to said seats. What is an argument worth, in any cause, when based on so weak a foundation as the rendering of two particles which have numberless meanings and shades of meanings, according to the connection in which they stand?

"The folly of resting so exclusive a claim, as Immersionists set up, upon two prepositions, must be manifest when we state that *eis* is used 1,730 times in the New Testament, and with,

perhaps, 100 different shades of meaning; and
that *ek* is used about 1,000 times, with fifty or
more different meanings."—*Miller.*

Third. But our opponents will say, Why
say they "went down *to* the water" and "came
up *from* the water," if no immersion took place?
We have a reason to give for the use of this
language, which we have not seen mentioned
by any of the many authors whose books we
have read on this subject. It is this: The eunuch "desired Philip that he should *come up*
and sit with him." Acts 8 : 31. The *coming up*
in this case plainly meant ascending to the seat
in the chariot. Now, when they *went down,*
they simply reversed the action of Philip, when
he went up; that is, they descended from the
seats in the chariot. This is the natural and
easy interpretation of the language, and is cor-
roborated by the fact that the evangelist spe-
cially mentions that "*both Philip and the eunuch*
went down." There must be a reason for spe-
cially stating that *they both* went down. That
reason is, that only Philip had been mentioned
as *coming up*, and when his action was reversed
it was done by both.

And it is stated that they both "came up," or ascended again to the seats in the chariot, as Philip had previously "come up." This statement, that they both ascended again into the chariot, is made in order to prepare for stating the scene which soon took place; namely, as they proceeded on the journey, suddenly "the Spirit of the Lord caught away Philip, that the eunuch saw him no more: and he (the eunuch) went on his way rejoicing." Acts 8 : 39.

The Greek verb, which is rendered "come up" in one of these verses, is the identical one which is rendered "come up" in the other. In one verse the action was certainly ascending to the seat in the chariot from the ground; of course it is the same in the other verse. This verb is *an-ebasan*, "come up." The verb which is rendered "went down" is the same simple verb, *ebasan*, with a different prefix, which reverses its action, namely, *kat-ebasan*, "went down." The action in the one case being simply that of ascending to the seat in the chariot, as we have shown that it certainly was, the action in the other was as certainly descending from the seat in the chariot—nothing more,

An unprejudiced reading of the Scriptural narrative will convince any one that this is a correct interpretation of the language and that the
much-abused "went down into the water" and
"come up out of the water" mean nothing more
nor less than that the two descended from seats
in the chariot to the water, and, after the baptism, resumed their seats in the chariot.

Fourth. What led the eunuch to think of
being baptized just at this time, was Philip's
preaching and opening to him the meaning of
the passage of Scripture, which he had just
been reading. In the third verse of the passage is the prophesy, "So shall he sprinkle
many nations." Isaiah 52 : 15. This, doubtless, Philip had explained to him. So that, so
far as mode is concerned, it was sprinkling,
which was in the mind of the eunuch, when he
asked baptism. Being a Jew, he was accustomed to sprinkling as the mode of purification,
and he could have expected nothing else than
to be baptized in that way. And had Philip
proceeded to baptize him by any other mode,
he would have had first to have explained to
him that the mode had been changed from that

predicted by the prophet and to which he was
accustomed as a Jew, and that immersion had
been substituted and the reasons for the change.
But the narrative, which details even small circumstances, gives no hint of any of all this having been done, for the reason that it was not
done: but Philip baptized him in accordance
with the prophesy.

Fifth. The statement is that this baptism
took place "in a desert." Acts 8 : 26. It was
not far from the place where Abraham and
Isaac were obliged to dig wells to get water for
their flocks; and "the herdmen of Gerar did
strive with Isaac's herdmen, saying, The water
is ours." Gen. 26 : 20. To presume that there
was a river or any considerable body of water
of any kind, sufficient for immersing, in this
desert, is but a fancy. The eunuch, it appears,
was rather surprised and pleased to find any
water in such a place. It was doubtless one of
those "springing waters" or "springs" in the
desert, mentioned Gen. 26 : 19, and boiling out
of the ground in a small quantity, afforded no
place for immersion. The Greek word translated *certain*—"a certain water"—is *ti*, which

does not indicate a well-known body or foun-
tain of water, as a scholar will at once compre-
hend: but *some* or *any* water. "They came to
some water," would be a strictly correct rendering. Also *ti* sometimes has the sense of a di-
minutive; and the rendering would also be correct were it, "They came to a *little* water."
The eunuch's expression, "See, here is water,"
literally translated, is, *Behold water*, and is a
form of expression which indicates a small
rather than a large amount of water.

The circumstances of this whole narrative indicate a place or region of but little water—"a
desert"—and the evangelist, guided by the
Spirit, protects us against the attacks of infidelity, by giving the details of the case. Had
he simply said, "And he baptized him," infidels
would have said, "It is a desert. Where was
the water? Did he baptize him in the chariot
or out of it? And, if in it, how did he get the
water there?" etc., etc. But, by giving the
particulars, that when *some*, or a *little* water,
was discovered they disembarked from the
chariot, procured the water and "he baptized
him," the mouth of infidelity is closed.

We have considered this, the third case of Christian baptism, at the greater length, from the fact that this is the only one of the nine cases in the New Testament to which Immersionists appeal for support for their visionary and proscribing theory.

CHAPTER VIII.

CHRISTIAN BAPTISM—PAUL.

The fourth case of Christian baptism in the sacred history is that of Paul. The record is as follows :

"And Ananias went his way, and entered into the house;· and putting his hands on him said, Brother Saul, the Lord, even Jesus, that appeared unto thee in the way as thou camest, hath sent me, that thou mightest receive thy sight, and be filled with the Holy Ghost. And immediately there fell from his eyes as it had been scales: and he received sight forthwith, and arose, and was baptized. And when he had received meat, he was strengthened."—Acts 9: 17-19.

And:

"And now why tarriest thou? arise, and be baptized."—Acts 22 : 16.

All we know about the mode of Paul's baptism is given in the above quotation. We ask the reader to candidly consider the language and decide for himself whether or not there is

any room for the supposition of immersion in
the case. Paul was in the house of one Judas,
in the city of Damascus. He was blind, weak-
ened and exhausted. When Ananias spoke to
him, he "forthwith received his sight, and arose,
and was baptized, and when he had received
meat, he was strengthened." Not one hint is
given about leaving the house for baptism and
again returning for "meat." The "receiving
sight," "arising," "being baptized" and "receiving meat," all occur in rapid succession
without removing from the spot where Ananias
found him.

The circumstances of this case preclude the
idea of immersion :

First It is not admissible to suppose that
the writer would narrate small and apparently
unimportant circumstances and yet would omit,
right in the midst of them, such a circumstance as
leaving the house before the train of circumstances was completed and going some distance in
search of a river or pool, and then returning to
the house for the completing of the train of circumstances. While this fact does not prove
positively that the baptism was not by immer-

sion, it is so strong a presumptive evidence against it, that it amounts to very little short of positive proof.

Second. It seems that Paul had grown weak under the prostrating effects of the scene through which he had passed and three days of fasting. Acts 9:9. Hence the statement that "when he had received meat, he was strengthened." The statement of his being strengthened seems to have been made for the purpose of calling attention to the fact that he had become weak, and his weakness must have been considerable to have been the subject of mention in the brief narrative. Now observe that his baptism took place before he was relieved from this weakness. Can any one suppose that the going out for the immersion of a subject in such condition and the return to the house, would be omitted by the evangelist from a narrative in which he gives even so small a particular as that "he arose?" The fact that nothing of the kind—not even a hint—occurs in the narrative, under the circumstances, precludes the possibility of immersion in this case.

Third. The command of Ananias was, "Arise,

and be baptized:" Paul "arose, and was
baptized." Now, in both these cases a word is
used which implies, not only that Paul was baptized in the house, but that he was *standing up*.
The word is *anastas*, which is the second aorist
participle of the verb *anistami*. This verb is
defined by the lexicons to mean "to stand up,
arise, rise up." The participle, *anastas*, is, therefore, "having stood up," etc. Ananias' command to Paul, therefore, when literally rendered, was, "having stood up, be baptized,"
and Paul's compliance was, "having stood up,
he was baptized."

The use of this participle in the New Testament not only shows that it means an upright
posture, but that the action performed by the
person rising followed immediately on his rising.
The following examples are given: The high
priest (*anastas*, having stood up) arose and said
unto them," Matt. 26:62; "Peter (*anastas*,
having stood up) arose in the midst of the disciples and said," Acts 1:15; "Then Paul (*anastas*, having stood up) stood up and beckoning
with his hand, said." Acts 13:16. These examples are sufficient to show to any considerate

reader that the use of this participle in the case of Paul's baptism indicates that the action of baptism followed immediately on his rising up and that it took place while he was in an erect posture. Was immersion ever performed in that way? Let us see how the Immersionist's definition of baptism, quoted in Chapter I, will fit the case—Ananias' command: " Having stood up, be dipped, once, backwards; "—Paul's compliance: "having stood up, he was dipped, once, backwards."

Dr. Armstrong, in his most convenient and scholarly book, " The Sacraments of the New Testament," issued this year (1880), quotes the following from Dr. J. H. Rice: " According to the idiom of the Greek language, these two words do not make two different commands, as the English reader would suppose, when he read 1, *arise;* 2, *be baptized.* But the participle (arise, literally, *standing up*) simply modifies the signification of the verb, or rather is used to complete the action of the verb, and, therefore, instead of warranting the opinion that Paul rose up, went out and was immersed, it definitely and precisely expresses his posture when he received baptism."

And yet, in spite of such circumstances as
are given by the sacred history, in the case of
the baptism of the great apostle, we are required to believe that immersion alone is baptism, the penalty of our incredulity being exclusion from the sacrament of the Lord's Supper
by one party of the Immersionists, and exclusion from the salvation of ·the Cross by the
other.

CHAPTER IX.

CHRISTIAN BAPTISM—CORNELIUS.

The fifth case of Christian baptism was of Cornelius and his friends, in his house in Cæsarea.

"While Peter yet spake these words, the Holy Ghost fell on all them which heard the word. And they of the circumcision which believed were astonished, as many as came with Peter, because that on the Gentiles also was poured out the gift of the Holy Ghost. For they heard them speak with tongues, and magnify God. Then answered Peter, Can any man forbid water, that these should not be baptized, which have received the Holy Ghost as well as we? And he commanded them to be baptized in the name of the Lord. Then prayed they him to tarry certain days."—Acts 10: 44-48.

Was this a case of immersion or aspersion? We think, the latter, clearly.

First. They were in a house, and the only natural interpretation of the language is that the baptism took place upon the spot; without leaving the house.

Second. Immediately on their receiving "the pouring out of the Holy Ghost," Peter, though not through with his discourse, said, "Can any man forbid water, that these should not be baptized?" These words were spoken in the house, and they plainly involve the request that the water should be brought in : certainly not that they should go out in search of it, or to it. Dean Alford says, "The article should here certainly be expressed, Can any forbid *the water* to these who have received the Spirit? The expression 'forbid' used with 'the water' is interesting, as showing that the practice was to *bring the water to the candidate, not the candidate to the water.*"

Third. Peter, in narrating this incident to his brethren, said :

"And as I began to speak, the Holy Ghost fell on them, as on us at the beginning. Then remembered I the word of the Lord, how that he said, John indeed baptized with water; but ye shall be baptized with the Holy Ghost."— Acts 11 : 15, 16.

Here Peter tells us clearly that the falling of the Holy Ghost on those in Cornelius' house and on the apostles in the "upper room" in Jerusalem on the day of Pentecost,—"on us at the beginning"—was *baptism* and that its counterpart is water baptism. The *falling* of the Holy Ghost on the people at once reminded him of the manner of John's baptism, and his pointed statement that it did so, settles the question of the mode of baptism practiced in this case, to the satisfaction of any one free from prejudice, and, as positively as so many words would do, declares John's baptism to have been by aspersion. And whoever claims that John's baptism was by immersion, takes issue with the inspired apostle, Peter.

Peter preached in the house: before his discourse was finished, the Holy Ghost was poured out upon Cornelius and others: Peter remembered that the Lord had said he would baptize with the Spirit as John baptized with water; he commanded water to be brought, and, accordingly, they were baptized in the house. This is the plain interpretation, and the only possible one, of this piece of sacred history.

CHAPTER X.

CHRISTIAN BAPTISM—LYDIA—THE JAILER.

The sixth case of Christian baptism was that of Lydia and her household, recorded at Acts 16 : 13-15. The scene was by the side of a river, whither the apostles went, not for the convenience of baptizing, but because it was a place where "prayer was wont to be made." Lydia and other women resorted to the same spot for the purpose of prayer. Lydia gave attention to the things spoken by Paul and she and her household were at once baptized.

There is nothing in this case which indicates the mode of the baptism, further than the fact, which is universal in the New Testament baptisms, that she received baptism immediately on accepting Christ and on the spot. Being away from her house and not having expected baptism, she was not prepared with change of garments, which would be necessary in case of immersion, and there is no intimation given of

any of the arrangements and delay necessary
for immersion. It can hardly be supposed that
the apostle would have omitted mention of
these details, while giving others of no greater
importance.

From the above considerations, and there
being nothing to the contrary, we conclude that
this case was like the others and that, while
Lydia and her household may have been baptized *with* the water of the river, they were not
baptized *in* it : but that the water " fell on
them " as in the baptism of the Holy Ghost.

THE JAILER AND HIS FAMILY.

The seventh case is recorded as follows :

" And they spake unto him the word
of the Lord, and to all that were in the
house. And he took them the same hour of
the night, and washed their stripes; and was
baptized, he and all his, straightway. And
when he had brought them into his house, he
set meat before them, and rejoiced, believing in
God with all his house."—Acts 16: 32-34.

The circumstances detailed in this account,
beginning at the 25th verse, plainly show that
immersion was out of the question. Let the

reader examine the account for himself and decide whether or not immersion was possible. Among other things consider the following :

First. The scene, including the baptism, took place at the hour of midnight. While the evangelist details apparently unimportant circumstances, not a hint is given of leaving the jail and going in search of a place for immersing, which would hardly have escaped mention had it taken place, especially if at midnight.

Second. The duty of the jailer was to keep prisoners "safely" and it was a violation of the law for him to allow them, under any circumstances, outside the prison walls. To do so was, by the law, a forfeiture of his own life. It can scarcely be supposed that this jailer would have violated the law, under such circumstances, by going out in company with the prisoners even for baptism. The exacting character of the law and his respect for and fear of it, are indicated by his determination to take his own life when he discovered that the prison doors were open.

Third. The baptism took place after their removal from "the inner prison," where they had been in stocks, and previous to their removal into the residence portion of the prison ; that is, in the "outer prison," or in that part of the prison where those were kept who were not "thrust into the inner prison and their feet made fast in stocks." Examine the Scripture narrative of the case and you will see that this is true.

Fourth. Paul said, about in so many words, that they had not been out of the prison during the night. "When it was day" the magistrates sent word to the jailer to release Paul and Silas "privily." But Paul refused to go out "privily," and required that the magistrates should themselves come and take them out, which they accordingly did. Now, whoever supposes that the apostles had been out "privily" during the night, supposes them guilty of extraordinary and unpardonable duplicity in professing an unwillingness to go out " privily."

EIGHTH AND NINTH CASES.

There are two other instances of Christian baptism by the apostles: Acts 18:7, 8, and Acts 19:1-5. In these cases there are no circumstances which indicate the mode of administration; except the absence of any information that they took place near to any pond or creek or that there was any delay or preparations for immersion. We are left, therefore, to infer that these baptisms were performed by the apostle Paul in the way that he himself was baptized and which is so strongly indicated in all the other cases as being the only way in which baptism was administered by the apostles.

We have now gone through and examined all the cases of Christian baptism recorded in the Acts of the Apostles. We have found that in some of them immersion was out of the question: in others highly improbable; and in not one of them do the circumstances point to immersion as the probable mode. The weight of evidence is overwhelmingly against the idea of immersion. It cannot be proven from the New Testament that the apostles ever immersed a single subject. Nor can it be proven that any one was ever immersed in the days of the apostles. We defy every Immersionist on earth to prove from Scripture that any person was ever immersed in the primitive Church. In addition to all other facts and arguments, the nature and design of Christian baptism prove that *affusion* or *sprinkling* was the mode.

Mr. Kurtz pertinently inquires and remarks: " Were all the disciples instructed and converted by Paul near to some pond or creek? If so, how singular it is, that converts, in these and other cases, could not be found, unless, by a remarkable coincidence, a large body of water was near! If all the ponds and creeks, which exist in the imagination of Immersionists who interpret the Acts of the Apostles, had really watered Judea, then, it may be proved by calculation, that there was water enough to have turned the whole land into a sea."

In the light of this survey of all the cases of Christian baptism in the New Testament, we commend to our readers the following catholic thoughts by Dr. Armstrong: " To require immersion in order to admission to the Church of God, is to infringe upon that 'liberty wherewith Christ hath made his people free,' and to 'teach for doctrine the commandments of men.' And to exclude from the Lord's table, the Lord's people, because they have not been immersed, is to bring upon the soul the guilt of the sin of schism."

Alexander Campbell, in summing up his arguments in favor of immersion, mentions this one: "The places where this rite was administered—*in rivers* and where there was much water." In this assertion there is a good deal of what is now-a-days familiarly called "*cheek*," not to use a word of worse meaning. Mr. Campbell knew that no river, nor much water, is mentioned in connection with any of the New Testament baptisms, John's only excepted. What will candid people think of a cause which must be propped up by such efforts to mislead the uninformed and credulous?

CHAPTER XI.

THE GREEK WORD BAPTIZO.

A great amount of time and labor have been spent in trying to arrive at a correct definition of the word *baptizo* as used in the Septuagint and the New Testament. Writers have for this purpose gone to the writings of the ancient Greek authors and to the Greek lexicons. We propose a different course, on the principle that the Bible is the best intepreter of itself and is by far the best dictionary for a definition of a word used by the sacred writers. Does the New Testament define the meaning of *baptizo* as used therein? It certainly does, and plainly. Let us see:

Here is the *prediction*, or *word :*

"Ye (the apostles) shall be *baptized* with the Holy Ghost."—Acts I : 5.

Let the reader bear in mind that all we are hunting just now is a clear definition of the Greek word *baptizo*.

Here is the definition:

"And there appeared unto them cloven tongues like as of fire, and it *sat upon* each of them. And they were all filled with the Holy Ghost."—Acts 2: 3, 4.

"The Holy Ghost *fell on* them, *as on us at the beginning."*—Acts 11 : 15.

"On the Gentiles also was *poured out* the gift of the Holy Ghost."—Acts 10: 45.

"That **they** might receive the Holy Ghost: for as yet he had *fallen on* none of them."— Acts 8: 15, 16.

"The Holy Ghost *fell on* all them which heard the word."—Acts 10: 44.

"The Holy Ghost; which he *shed on* us abundantly."—Titus 3 : 6.

From the above the reader will see that the *infallible* dictionary defines the word *baptizo* in the *prediction* or *promise*, by the following words in the fulfillment: "fell on, poured out, shed on." Now who dare take issue with the infallible lexicon? And who needs to go to the Greek classics and lexicographers for a definition of a Bible word when the Bible itself plainly furnishes it?

Our Immersionist friends complain very much

that the word *baptizo* is not translated, but is transferred from the Greek, simply. But this complaint comes back on them also, like Pyrrhus' elephant, for when they get it changed to their notion, as they do in the book, which is the issue of the labors of the mouse of the American Bible Union, they have it *immerse*, which is only a *transferred* Latin word, as every scholar knows. It is *immersum* anglicized. And the elephant bears down hardest on the return trip, for *baptize* has been in use in the English language hundreds of years longer than *immerse*. *Baptize* appears in the Geneva Bible, translated in 1557: in Cranmer's Bible, 1539: in Tyndale's Bible, 1534; and in Wickliff's translation in 1380. *Immerse* appears first in the English language in the writings of Lord Bacon, who was born in 1561! So *baptize* is the older English word by more than 181 years! According to Immersionists, English lexicographers *cannot* define *baptize*, because *baptize* is an anglicized Greek word. But English lexicographers *can* define *immerse*, although *immerse* is an anglicized Latin word, which has been in the language centuries less time than *baptize!*

Sample of reason: Johnson says "to baptize is to sprinkle," and Webster defines baptism to be "the application of water to the person." There is where the shoe pinches!

This is a suitable place to introduce what Peter Edwards, the author, called "a case" and modestly presented in his pointed little book published in 1841:

"Before I enter on the Mode of Baptism, I would take the liberty of proposing to my Baptist friends a plain case; not so much a case of conscience as a case of criticism. That on which this case is founded is as follows: It is well known that under the present dispensation there are two instituted ordinances; the one in Scripture is expressed by the term *deipnon*, a supper, the other by *baptisma*, baptism. The proper and obvious meaning of *deipnon* is a feast or a common meal, Mark 6:21; the proper meaning of *baptisma* is said to be the immersion of the whole body. The case then is this:

"If, because the proper meaning of the term *baptisma*, baptism, is the immersion of the whole body, a person, who is not immersed, cannot be said to have been baptized, since nothing short of immersion amounts to the full import of the word baptism. If this be true, I should be glad to know that as *deipnon*, a supper, properly means a feast or common meal, whether a person who, in the use of that ordinance, takes only a piece of bread of half an inch square, and drinks a table-spoonful of wine, which is neither a feast nor a common meal, and so does not come up to the proper meaning of the word, can be said to have received the Lord's supper."

Mr. Edwards modestly called the above "a case:" we name it a *poser.*

We also favor the reader with the following from Dr. Guthrie's Pedobaptist's Guide:

"THE SYRIAC RENDERING OF 'BAPTIZO.'

"One of the strongest conceivable arguments in favor of our view of 'baptizo' is to be found in a particular usage to which, as yet, I have made no allusion. We are apt unreflectingly to assume, from its occurrence in the original Greek of the four Gospels, that 'baptizo' was the identical word used by John the Baptist and our Lord. But very clearly it was not; for the language at that time spoken in Palestine was a modification of the ancient Hebrew, closely resembling the Syriac. Now the oldest version of the New Testament is the Syriac, which is believed to have been made in the first century. It is therefore in the highest degree probable that the Syriac translators would employ the very term to denote baptism which had been employed by John the Baptist, Christ, and the Apostles, in their vernacular Syro-Chaldaic, and which would be well known throughout Palestine and the adjacent provinces of Syria. What word, then, do the Syriac translators employ? A word meaning to dip? No. The Syriac, of course, has such a word : but never once in that venerable version is it used to denote baptism. Instead of it, the word used is the verb 'to stand,' in the Aphel, or causative conjugation (corresponding to the Hiphel in Hebrew); so that the Syriac—and therefore probably the original—word 'to baptize' means literally and primarily 'to cause or make stand.' However this may be explained, it goes directly against the Immersionist. If it is to be explained modally, it will prove that the mode of baptism was not to immerse the subject, but to make him stand (as is represented in ancient pictures), and have the baptismal element poured on his head. In this case, we may discern a peculiar significance in the words of the Syrian disciple Ananias, when he said to Paul, '*Arise*, and be baptized.' If it is to be explained more generally in the sense of 'constituting,' 'confirming,' or conferring a recognized standing, it is no less fatal to the Immersionist theory; for then it is a generic term, without reference to mode, which the Syriac translators (after the inspired men whose word we assume it probable they adopted) did not deem it of the slightest consequence to indicate. This is an argument not much used in the Baptismal controversy, as popularly conducted; but it is one whose force will appear the more it is pondered, and which the Immersionist will find it a hard task to explain away."

Of the Syriac version Calmet's Dictionary says: "In the third century it already was the authoritative version of the Church." Being the oldest translation of the New Testament in the world, it is an important witness, and one to which Immersionists cannot object, for it was made in the first century, when, if their exclusive views are correct, immersion was universally praticed as the only Christian baptism. We quote again; this time from Dr. N. L. Rice:

"1st. It is a remarkable fact, that the primary meaning of the word *amad*, which is uniformly employed in the Syriac version to translate *baptizo*, is *to stand*, and then *to cause to stand*, or *confirm*. This is the meaning of the word in Hebrew, Chaldaic and Arabic, which are very near of kin of the Syriac. The Lexicons all give the word this derivation. 'It is hardly credible,' says Professor Stuart, 'that the Syriac word could vary so much from all these languages, as properly to mean *immerse, dip*."

"2d. Besides, the Syriac has a word (*tseva*) which properly means to dip or plunge; and this word is used in every case in the New Testament, where the idea of dipping occurs. But it is not used in translating *baptizo*. How shall we account for the fact, that instead of using the word signifying to *immerse*, in translating *baptizo*, the Syriac translator uniformly employs a word meaning *to confirm?*

"Now, then, when we remember, that the Syriac has a word which signifies properly to *dip*, how shall we account for the fact that the translator rendered *baptizo* by a word meaning to *confirm*, to *purify*, to *enlighten*, and which does not express *mode?* It will not be pretended that he was swayed by Pedobaptist influence; since if our Immersionist friends are in the right, there were then no Pedobaptists in the world. Most evidently, the Syriac translator did not understand *baptizo* as meaning to *immerse*, or he would have chosen a Syriac word which has this meaning."

When, therefore, we are required to be immersed or else be pronounced unbaptized, we simply reply, that there is no warrant in Scripture for such ritual dogmatism: nor have Immersionists all the authority and knowledge there is in the whole of Greekdom.

CHAPTER XII.

DESIGN AND USE OF BAPTISM.

There are two essential facts in the history of salvation, viz: The work of the eternal Son, and the work of the eternal Spirit—the death of Christ as an atonement for sin, and the application of the merits of his death in the purification or regeneration of the human heart. Both of these works are essential to salvation and nothing else is essential.

Both these essential facts have ever been represented by types. In the New Testament there are two sacraments: the Lord's supper and baptism. One of these represents the first and the other the second of these facts. The Lord's supper is to stand perpetually as an emblem of the death of Christ, and baptism as an emblem of the purification of the human heart. Now, whoever claims that baptism represents the "death, burial and resurrection of Christ," makes both the sacraments represent one of the essential facts and leaves the other without representation.

The uses of baptism may be enumerated as follows:

1. It is a *sacrament* or *oath* of fidelity.   We take it in arranging ourselves on the side of Christ.   It binds its subjects to an obligation of fidelity to God.

2. It is a mark of *religious distinction.*   The Jews were distinguished from the Gentiles by circumcision.   The Christians, or subjects of baptism, are by it distinguished and separated from the general mass of irreligious men.

3. It is a sign of spiritual blessings.   In representing primarily the work of the Holy Ghost in regenerating the heart, it generically signifies the whole work of grace in the soul,—pardon, regeneration, sanctification, etc.: in short the whole work of salvation as carried forward in the soul and consummated by the Holy Ghost.

4. It is the *seal* of the new covenant.   God has always affixed a *seal* or *token* to his covenants.   Circumcision was the seal of the old covenant, "*a token of the covenant*" between God and Abraham.   The gospel is the Abrahamic covenant completely developed, and comprehends all nations and extends through

all time. What circumcision was under the old, baptism is under the new dispensation:— a seal of the covenant of salvation which God has graciously made with man.

CONCLUDING REMARKS.

1. Let us admit, for argument, that baptizo, in classic use, means to immerse, which cannot be shown, and also allow the Immersionists' claim that, therefore, it ought to be translated *immerse* everywhere in Scripture. A rule which is good in one case is good in every parallel one. Now let us try this rule on a parallel case: Circumcision is a word which means in the Greek "to cut round." It came to the English through Rome and there got a Latin form and is a *transferred* word. The same rule which requires that baptism, according to the Immersionists' claim, be translated *immerse*, requires that circumcision be translated *cutting around.*

Now let us see them try it on a few passages: " In whom also ye are *cut around* with the *cutting around* made without hands:"—" For we are the *cutting around* which worship God in the Spirit:"—" And *cutting around* is that of the heart." The translation theory will not work.

2. At the memorable time of the passage of the Red Sea, there was, according to Scripture, one baptism and one immersion. Of the baptism the Isaelites were the subjects, (see I Cor. 10: 1, 2): "All our fathers were under the cloud, and all passed through the sea; and were all baptized unto Moses in the cloud and in the sea." And according to Moses their baptism took place on "dry ground," (see Ex. 14: 29): "But the children of Israel walked upon dry land in the midst of the sea; and the waters were a wall unto them on their right hand, and on their left;" and according to David it was by "pouring out" the water, (see Psalm 77: 17): "The clouds poured out water." Of the immersion the Egyptians were the subjects, (see Ex. 14: 28): "And the waters returned, and covered the chariots, and the horsemen, and all the host of Pharaoh that came into the sea after them; there remained not so much as one of them."

Here then, by the express testimony of Scripture, we are taught that *baptism* is one thing and *immersion* another. The *baptism* of the one party consisted in their escaping the *immersion*, and the party *immersed* was the one that was not baptized: But "Israel (the *baptized* party) saw the Egyptians (the *immersed* party) dead upon the sea-shore."

In conclusion, I will say to the patient reader, that I have endeavored to be as concise as possible. What I have given are only samples of the arguments which may be produced to show that the Scriptural mode of water baptism is the same as the Scriptural mode of Spiritual baptism, viz : *the falling of the element on the subject* Very many of the arguments have not been so much as mentioned in these few pages. For them the reader must seek larger books.

If I have succeeded in undeceiving one individual, who stood in danger of being misled by unfounded, though confident, assertions, I am amply paid for the labor of writing. I confidently commit this book to the care of the Great Head of the Church, praying, that he will pardon whatever in it is human, and bless whatever is agreeable to his will to the firm and happy establishment of the reader in "the faith once delivered to the saints."

www.ingramcontent.com/pod-product-compliance
Lightning Source LLC
Chambersburg PA
CBHW022343020726
47500CB00004B/1254

* 9 7 8 3 3 3 7 3 9 2 6 9 7 *